The O Murder

Geoffrey L. Lefavi

Published by Geoffrey L. Lefavi, 2024.

This is a work of fiction. Similarities to real people, places, or events are entirely coincidental.

THE O MURDER

First edition. February 1, 2024.

Copyright © 2024 Geoffrey L. Lefavi.

ISBN: 979-8224141579

Written by Geoffrey L. Lefavi.

Table of Contents

The O Murder

Dedication

To my dance partner, who pushed me into writing fiction.

Introduction

In a shocking turn of events, a once serene small town has plunged into utter chaos, reeling from the aftermath of three citizens being shot in a single day.

As the State Police delve into the investigation, they are confronted with a daunting challenge — the unsettling realization that there is an overwhelming abundance of potential culprits.

The list of individuals under scrutiny has ballooned to over seventy, creating a perplexing puzzle for law enforcement.

In their quest for answers, the State Police attempt to untangle the intricate web of activities within Gomorrah (actual name: Greenview).

Who orchestrates these events, and what motives drive their actions? The once-quiet town now echoes with uncertainty as residents anxiously await the revelation of the truth behind the chaos that has gripped their community.

Suspicions run rampant among the townspeople and the state police. The state police oversee the investigation. The main help is a woman known for being a blabbermouth by the townspeople.

Lies upon lies build a case that could not be true. Not being from Greenview makes it harder for the state police to determine who to believe and who to arrest.

Chapter 1: Going Home

Turk is a slaughterer; he kills cows for a slaughterhouse. After having a physical confrontation with a manager, he was sent to a psychologist. The psychologist said he had psychological symptoms experienced by many slaughterhouse employees as a form of trauma disorder, such as Post-Traumatic Stress Disorder (PTSD). He was ordered to take a week off. If his attitude did not change, he would be terminated.

Turk could not drive to his home; the snow was too deep. He parked by the side of the highway; it was a quarter-mile hike up the hill to his home.

Turk has been hiking for what seems like forever. As he stands on the field, perplexed and surrounded by the seemingly unending expanse of snow, he begins to feel a growing unease. The blizzard, which initially seemed like any other winter storm, now takes on an eerie quality. The snowfall muffles the usual sounds of nature and sounds from the highway, creating an almost surreal silence broken only by the occasional howling wind.

With each step, Turk becomes increasingly disoriented. The landscape, once familiar, transforms into a white, featureless maze. The biting cold starts to gnaw at him, penetrating even through his layered clothing. He pulls his scarf tighter and presses on, determined to reach his home.

A sudden loud noise. Turk turns around, expecting to see a moose. He sees nothing. He notices the trail he created walking in the snow was a big "O." He has been walking in a circle. Fear enters his mind, taking over for a minute as he stands in the snow. With his home in sight, he takes three or four steps, checking his home location. Takes another three or four steps. Rechecks his location. He repeats this until he reaches his home.

He can feel the weight of fatigue settling in as the cold seeps into his bones.

Turk finally reaches his home. He opens the door and calls out Sandy, his common-law wife's name. No response. She should be home; the blizzard would have kept her from going anywhere.

The fireplace's fire is almost out. He runs over to the fireplace and neatly places three logs into the fireplace. As he warms his hands from the fire, he wonders where Sandy could be.

Turk heads over to the kitchen entrance to check the clipboard, where they leave messages for each other. No messages.

He looks into the kitchen and sees red paint on the kitchen cabinets. He enters the kitchen and sees a big red circle painted on the cabinet. He walks over to the kitchen cabinet and touches the paint; he is afraid it is not paint.

He starts calling out "Sandy" over and over again, running around their home.

Out of breath, sanity comes back to his brain. He pulls out his cell phone and calls the sheriff. He tells the sheriff that Sandy is missing. That there is blood on the cabinets. And the fire in the fireplace is almost out.

The sheriff says not to touch anything and sit in the middle of the room on the floor. Turk says he is hungry. The sheriff says I will bring you something to eat; do not touch anything.

Turk says the driveway up the hill is snowed in. The sheriff says that is not a problem; Jack, the snowplow guy, is here; I'll have him create a path up the hill.

Sheriff Smith sends Jack to make a path up to Turk's home. Jack immediately leaves. He gets into his truck and takes a swig of whisky. He goes through a bottle every day. Jack does not like working in the snow and cold. It is an important job, keeping the roads open. He always tells himself, "It feeds the family."

The sheriff then calls the state police and asks them to immediately send a forensic team to Turk's home. The sheriff is well known, so he gets an immediate response from the forensic department.

Sheriff Smith is the sheriff of Greenview, a town with just three hundred people. The sheriff knows almost everybody by name and where they live.

The sheriff puts on his parka and tells his only deputy to watch the office. The sheriff grunts, not pleased having to go out into a blizzard.

The sheriff arrives at the driveway leading to Turk's home. It looks like Jack is almost done creating a path to the house. The sheriff spots Turk's truck. He pulls out his flashlight and climbs into the truck. He searches under and behind the seat and the glove box. Nothing interesting.

If Sheriff Smith had found something, he would have to devise an excuse for searching the truck without a warrant. It's not a problem; a small town gets small-town justice.

Jack comes down the hill and tells the sheriff he should be able to get up the hill. The sheriff thanked Jack and asked him to widen the pathway since several vehicles would arrive in the next hour.

The sheriff realizes that he forgot to get food for Turk. The sheriff runs to the restaurant and orders about three times what Turk will need.

Back at the hill, the sheriff easily drives to Turk's cabin.

The sheriff grabs the food and a tray he had in his trunk. He walks into the cabin without knocking. Turk is sitting on the floor where the sheriff told him to sit.

The sheriff sits the tray on the floor next to Turk and the food next to the tray.

The sheriff says, "Sorry about this situation. Please eat as much as you can. Then, we will go over everything that has happened today.

Turk, a burly individual, indulged in his favorite pastime—devouring copious amounts of junk food. The enticing aroma of greasy delights filled the air as he voraciously grabbed a bag; the ripping paper signaled the imminent feast.

Turk's appetite seemed insatiable. The delectable mix of salty and sweet, pushed to his taste buds by lard, found a new home in his ever-expanding belly, playfully defying the constraints of his straining belt.

The room was filled with the rhythmic cadence of Turk's munching, accompanied by the occasional delighted exclamation. His culinary adventure was a spectacle of unapologetic indulgence.

Finished with one bag of food, Turk starts to grab another. "Hold on," exclaims the Sheriff; he does not want to make Turk sick. He says let us talk, and if you are still hungry, you can eat some more later.

Turk sits there waiting for the sheriff to say something. The sheriff stands up and says, " Let me walk around your place, then we can talk.

The sheriff stares at the kitchen cabinet with the red circle for at least one minute. He moves through Turk's home, deliberately looking at each item in the cabin.

The sheriff sits on the floor at a ninety-degree angle to Turk. From an interrogation course he took from the FBI, he learned that seated directly across from a person creates a confrontational setting.

Currently, the sheriff does not want to accuse Turk of anything. He wants just a friendly conversation. The sheriff says to describe your day starting with when you got out of bed.

Turk says he got out of bed, dressed, and drove home.

The sheriff almost shouts, "Stop! Where did you sleep last night, and with whom?"

Turk says, "As a gentleman, I can't say with whom I slept."

The sheriff says it looks like a crime has been committed here. Tell me, or I will through your ass in jail.

Turk says, "Lisa Wineheart."

The sheriff shouts, "Isn't she married?"

Turk says, "Yep, but she treats me really good, and her husband has to go out of town frequently." Turk gives a slight giggle, which only adults do when they are talking about sex.

"Does her husband know you have been sleeping with her?"

"No, he ain't very smart."

"How about Sandy, your wife? Does she know?"

"She does not care. I think she may have her own piece of ass."

"Who?"

"No idea."

The unsettled sheriff says, "So this may not be a crime scene. It might be a horny unfulfilled wife going off with someone better."

"Maybe, but I need somebody to fix me dinner." Turk seemed more concerned about Sandy's cooking talent than the fact that she was missing.

The sheriff was about to grab the remaining two bags of food and head out the door when there was a knock at the door. The sheriff lets in the forensic team. He points to Turk and says get a DNA sample and fingerprints from him, then run a DNA scan of the red circle in the kitchen. Try to find something with the wife's fingerprints. Try to find DNA from something the wife used. She is missing, possibly a victim, or she ran off.

The sheriff feels good, like he is back at his old job as a captain in the Chicago Police Department. He retired from the CPD.

When he first started retirement, he went golfing every day. After a month, he was beginning to get bored playing golf. He was a poor golfer, and winter was coming soon, which prevented people from playing golf in the snow. A seasoned golfer reported that using bright orange golf balls did not help find the ball if the snow was on the ground.

After a year of doing nothing, he took a job as sheriff to give him something to do.

The forensic team looks like a bunch of ants running everywhere.

The sheriff asked how long until we get the DNA results. He was told one week. He wondered if and when the owner could live in the cabin. He was told they would be done in two hours, and after that, the place was his.

The sheriff tells Turk to stay put for the next two hours. If you stay put, you can have the other two bags of food. Turk gleefully shouts, "Yes!"

The sheriff heads back to his office. He was annoyed by having to interact with a slug like Turk.

The sheriff fills in his deputy at his office on what is happening at Turk's place. He asks his deputy if we have someone with all the gossip for our village.

The deputy says, "You are looking for Miss Emma Johnson."

The sheriff says to have her come here; we must talk to her.

Chapter 2: Office Work

A large part of police work is paperwork. Police spend much more time sitting than we do running after criminals. This is why the number one cause of death for police officers is heart attack. Police spend the whole day sitting in their patrol car. A crime happens; they jump out of a patrol car and keel over from a heart attack.

The sheriff calls Lisa Wineheart Turk's love interest. Lisa answers the phone. He identifies himself and asks if her husband is home.

Lisa says her husband is out of town. He says this conversation is confidential; no one will know what you tell me. Lisa says she understands.

"Turk was with you last night?"

"Yes."

"When did he leave?"

"This morning?"

"Do you know who Sandy was seeing?"

"No"

"Thank you. That is all I needed to know. This conversation never happened."

They hang up.

The deputy tells the sheriff that Miss Emma Johnson will arrive in thirty minutes. Ten minutes later, Miss Johnson showed up at the sheriff's office.

The sheriff sits down with Miss Johnson. "Do you know who Sandy, Turk's wife, was dating?"

"Yes."

"Who?"

"Why?"

"Sandy is missing; if something happened to her, it is my business. Otherwise, it is none of my business if she ran off with someone."

"Your deputy."

The sheriff writes down something. He looks up; he is shot in the chest. He falls to the floor, barely alive. Another shot hits Miss Johnson in the head. Slumped on the floor, she is dead.

The deputy ran out of the office a moment later and drove away.

Michael York, walking by, saw what happened and called 911.

Laying on the floor, unable to move, the sheriff thinks that in twenty-eight years with the CPD, he has never been shot or injured. Maybe he will move back to Chicago.

Michael York walks into the office while still talking to 911. He tells them that there is one dead and one severely injured. He was told ten minutes until an ambulance got there. He tells the sheriff that the ambulance will be here in ten minutes. The sheriff is unable to respond.

Michael York sits on the floor beside the sheriff and says, "Everything will be all right." The sheriff thinks, "I need a doctor, but I got a comedian."

Multiple sirens are heard in the distance. It is no longer snowing, so the sirens can be heard; the falling snow does not silence them.

Almost as fast as the state police and ambulances get there, a crowd forms outside the sheriff's office. The blizzard has let up, which means the whole town might show up. Nothing happens in a small town, usually.

The paramedics start IVs of plasma and D5W. The sheriff was in the ambulance within two minutes of the arrival of the paramedics and ambulance. The populace shouts words of encouragement as the ambulance pulls away.

Miss Johnson, the blabbermouth, is put in a body bag in a first-call car. As the car pulled away, there was total silence in reverence to the passing of Miss Emma Johnson.

Chapter 3: Hospital

The people of Greenview stood under the noonday sun, the blizzard a distant memory. Nobody moved for several minutes after the ambulance left with Sheriff Smith. Tears ran down everyone's face. Catastrophe seldom befalls Greenview. Unsure of what to do, they moved to the sidewalk and quietly talked to one another.

As the ambulance raced to the hospital, the ER staff were alerted that a GSW (gunshot wound) was coming.

The sheriff's labored breaths resonated in the confined space of the ambulance, a reminder of the fragility of human life.

The hospital staff stood ready to receive Sheriff Smith. The automatic doors swung open, admitting the wounded lawman into the sterile corridors of Huntington General. The urgency of the situation painted a grim scene against the white walls.

Dr. Emily Anderson, the seasoned chief surgeon, met the gurney with a calm intensity in her eyes. Her skilled hands wasted no time assessing the severity of the sheriff's wound. The operating room, a sanctuary against the chaos outside, awaited the critical task of extracting the bullet lodged in the sheriff's chest.

The Sheriff's clothing was cut off while giving security the Sheriff's guns and badge, to be kept in a secure vault. The security guard spoke to the sheriff, saying, "I'll take good care of these for you. The doctors here are great."

As Sheriff Smith was wheeled into the operating room, the harsh glare of overhead lights painted the scene in stark clarity. The rhythmic beeping of monitoring equipment, the hushed instructions between the medical team, and the sheriff's labored breaths created a symphony of urgency.

Dr. Anderson and her team embarked on the delicate dance to save a life.

The portable X-ray used in the OR showed a bullet lodged next to his heart, which may have pierced the heart. The state's best cardiologist works at this hospital. He was called in to help with the delicate surgery.

Now, in the sterile confines of the hospital, the battle against the shadows began—a struggle that would determine not only Sheriff Smith's fate but also the resilience of a town thrust into the unforgiving grip of violence—having two murders and one attempted murder in a single day.

The life-saving duo swiftly and delicately attacked the evil within. A state trooper watched from above in the observation room.

The sheriff's heartbeat, monitored, echoed the community's collective hope that the small hole in his heart would be mended.

The surgery neared its conclusion, marked by a collective exhale from the medical team. The small hole, once a threat to life, had been skillfully repaired. Though weakened by the ordeal, Sheriff Smith had a good chance of seeing another sunrise.

Dr. Anderson looked up at the trooper and gave a thumbs-up. The Sheriff was in critical condition, but he would get better unless there were any unexpected complications.

The Trooper talked to the surgeons after they completed the surgery. The trooper calls Lt. Jackson and says that the doctors talk in circles and that he was told the sheriff will get better unless he gets worse.

Lt. Jackson assured him that that is how all doctors talk. The Lieutenant assigns the trooper to watch over the sheriff. And he will send another trooper to help. If his condition changes, give him a call immediately. Hopefully, he will get better and be able to tell us who did the shooting.

Chapter 4: State Police

The State Troopers set up a command post in the sheriff's office. They ask everyone to clear the office. Michael York says, "I saw what happened." A universal "Huh" permeates the room.

There is a slight smile on Lieutenant Jackson's face; the lead trooper asks Mr. York to sit in a side office. He says forensics need room to do their job. Lt. Jackson sits in the office with Mr. York and asks him to tell him what he saw.

Mr. York pauses a few seconds, then says, "The blizzard was still pretty intense, so I hugged the building to stay out of the wind. Movement in the sheriff's office caught my eye. I looked in the window and saw Miss Johnson talking to the sheriff. There were no shouts, just two gunshots. I debated whether I should go into the office to help. As I dialed my phone, the deputy ran out the office door, got into his patrol car, and took off. I had not seen the deputy in the office before the shooting. I do not know where he was. I did not see anyone else in the building. I called 911 and entered the building. Miss Johnson was dead, and the sheriff was in bad shape."

Lt. Jackson asked why he was out in a blizzard. Mr. York said he was going to eat at the restaurant. Being cooped up in his apartment during a prolonged storm is tedious, especially in this town, which is always dull.

Lt. Jackson asks Mr. York if he touched anything. Mr. York said, "Only the door. I sat down next to the Sheriff, trying to comfort him."

Lt. Jackson asks, "Did the sheriff say anything?"

"No, I do not think he was capable of talking. I just told him the ambulance would be here in ten minutes. After that, I just sat there."

Lt. Jackson asks, "Why did you sit there?"

"I was afraid that the sheriff would die. I did not want him to die alone. Everybody needs somebody at a time like this, so I felt I had no option but to keep the sheriff company."

Lt. Jackson asks, "Would you mind staying here for about an hour in case we think of any further questions?"

Mr. York says, "I am hungry. Would you mind if I got some takeout from the restaurant and immediately returned here?"

Lt. Jackson says, "That is fine. I will send a trooper along with you to protect our only witness." Lt. Jackson did not want him running off if he turned out to be a suspect.

Lt. Jackson tells Mr. York and the trooper not to discuss the case. We want to avoid alerting the bad guy about our actions. They leave for the restaurant.

Lt. Jackson looks around the sheriff's offices. He notes a back door. He tells the fingerprint people to thoroughly check the back door for prints, though most people in this weather will wear gloves. He tells another forensic person to check for footprints by the back door. Use the front door and walk around to the back door. We do not want to mess up any footprints on the ground.

Lt. Jackson looks at the two-way radio sitting on a desk. He thinks out loud; I wonder if he would answer a call.

The forensic people tell the Lieutenant to go ahead and use it; the radio has been printed.

Just then, Mr. York and the escort return with a couple of bags of food.

Mr. York says, "Mary normally closes the restaurant at 8 pm. If you like, she will stay open as long as you need; call her. Here is her number."

Lt. Jackson says thank you. He then asks what is name of the deputy.

Mr. York says, "Herbert Swanson. His nickname is Herb."

Chapter 5: Lieutenant Samuel Jackson

Lieutenant Samuel Jackson had recently earned the rank of Lieutenant, a hard-earned achievement after dedicating a decade of service to the State Police. Fueled by ambition, he saw this promotion as a stepping stone on the fast track toward the coveted rank of Captain.

However, Lieutenant Jackson's rising career brought a shadow of concern into his household. His wife, Peggy, harbored a deep unease about his role in the State Police. The grim realities of the job had left her haunted by the fear that harm could befall her husband while on duty. The echoes of tragedy resonated in her mind as she witnessed two of Samuel's friends lose their lives in the line of duty.

As Lieutenant Jackson basked in the glow of his recent promotion, Peggy's fear cast a somber undertone over their celebrations. The duality of pride and fear permeated their home, creating a delicate balance between professional achievements and the harsh realities of life in law enforcement.

The Lieutenant was excited when he received his assignment to the Greenview case.

His wife showed despair. When he told Peggy about the three shootings, one person was the sheriff.

The Lieutenant told Peggy not to fear; the sheriff was just a hick town sheriff with no real police training, contrasting it with his team of ten to twenty troopers, adaptable to the demands of the case.

Though not pleased, Peggy reluctantly acquiesced with an uneasy "OK."

The Lieutenant packed his bag, getting ready to bring justice to the small hick town.

As he left, he told his wife he would give her a call every day and that this case would take little time to solve. Peggy knew she would only get calls occasionally; he would be too busy with work.

The Lieutenant's father had been a sergeant in the Springfield police department. He and Samuel never got along. Samuel's attitude was he was more intelligent than his father. His father was mad because he knew Samuel was more intelligent than him.

His mother was the first person he called when he was made lieutenant. His mother said she was pleased and proud of his achievement, although she feared for his life since he took too many chances while performing his duties.

Samuel never talked to his father. His mother tried many times to fix their relationship. His mother told Samuel he would be a much better officer, i.e., he took advantage of his father's experience.

She told his father that Samuel was his son. Please let him get to know you before it is too late.

They were just too stubborn.

His father constantly checked on how Samuel was doing in the force. He never told anyone he was keeping track.

Chapter 6: Who Shot Turk

Lt. Jackson picks up the two-way microphone and says, "Herb, are you there? Come back. Are you out there, Herb? Please come back. Herb, this is Lieutenant Jackson of the state police. Please come back."

Frustrated with no response, the Lieutenant gave it one more call. "We need your help to find the guy that shot the sheriff."

Static, a voice comes over the radio, "I'm going to get this guy myself. I'm sure I know who it is, but I have to collect enough evidence to convict him."

Lt. Jackson says, "We are here to help you collect evidence. How do you think the sheriff would feel if the bad guy killed you? Come to the sheriff's office, and let's get this guy together. You are the lead in this case. Let us help you."

"It looks like the bad guy entered the office by the back door. Is that door usually locked? If so, who has a key?" Static, no answer. "We need your help!" Static, no answer. "What case was the sheriff working on? We can find no paperwork on it." Static, no response.

Lt. Jackson orders his staff, "Look for the latest case the sheriff was working on." The bluff to the deputy did not work, but maybe it could be a good lead.

Lt. Jackson called headquarters, asking if we have the equipment to triangulate a two-way radio signal. He is told, "No." He then asks if there is a friend in the military who could help us locate a radio signal. He was told that they would ask around.

The fingerprint people have returned to their office to run the collected fingerprints through the FBI database. If they work fast, they may have a result in about a day or so.

Lt. Jackson says, "I just got a report saying that the sheriff is doing better, but he will be in the hospital for a long time." Static, no response.

Lt. Jackson tells his staff, "Call the hospital and ensure they do not give out a status report on the sheriff. Call headquarters have two troopers in a plain car go to the hospital and stake out the sheriff's room beside the two troopers already watching the sheriff. They should dress up like doctors or janitors.

A trooper hands Lt. Jackson the paperwork the sheriff was working on when he got shot. It is a missing person report on Sandy, the wife of Turk. It looks like both of them liked to play around.

Two troopers are sent to talk to Turk to see if his wife has returned or if he has communicated with her. The troopers are warned that Turk is a suspect in a murder case. Be careful.

Driving to the Turk's cabin, the troopers approach a car at the bottom of the hill to Turk's cabin. They notice that it is the Deputy's car and keep going.

Out of sight of the deputy's car, the trooper calls the Lieutenant, telling him they did not have a chance to interview Turk since the deputy was parked at the bottom of the hill.

Three more state troopers' cars are sent to be close to the deputy (within a quarter mile).

Lt. Jackson gets on the sheriff's old analog two-way radio and starts shouting, "You horses ass. If we had not wasted time trying to find you, Turk would have been in custody hours ago."

"Deputy Herbert Swanson, my cars have you surrounded. You can work with us, or we can put you under arrest for interfering with an investigation. What would your Highness like?"

The deputy says, OK, what would you like me to do?" Lt. Jackson asks, "Do you have a line of sight of the cabin?" The deputy says yes. "Move your car so Turk cannot see you.

The deputy moves his car. Within a minute, a trooper knocks on the passenger side door, and then he gets into his car. The trooper says, my partners will secretly hike up the hill so they can give us cover fire if Turk starts shooting. They will call us when they are in position. Then we will drive up the hill in your patrol car and knock on his door.

A few minutes later, a trooper called, saying they were in position. He leaves the phone in speaker mode so they can hear what is going on.

The trooper says to the deputy, "Let's go. You will do the talking, and I will stand behind you with my gun drawn. If anything terrible happens, drop to the floor so I can get a clear shot. Ask Turk about his wife, if she is there, and if he has talked to her. If Turk invites us in, I will put my gun in my pocket and still hold it with my finger on the trigger."

The deputy knocks on the door. Turk peeks through the window, then shouts, "What do you want, deputy?"

The deputy says he is here to talk to him about his wife. Then he says could you open the door? It is cold out here.

Turk to go away. The deputy says that is not possible; this is a criminal investigation. It would be best if you opened the door. The place is surrounded. If I tell them to break down the door, you will probably be killed. Please open the door.

The trooper behind the deputy bends down and whispers into his phone, "Get a warrant."

"Please, Turk. The troopers here want to walk down the hill and get into their warm cars. Let us sit down and talk. Open the door, and make sure you do not have a gun in your hand. Speak to me, Turk."

From inside the cabin, a gunshot is heard. The trooper shouts, "A gunshot inside. Check for other doors."

The deputy starts pounding on the door, yelling, "Open the door, Open the Door."

A latch on the front door is thrown. The trooper shouts, "Activity at the front door."

The door opens, and it is Sandy, Turk's wife. She is holding a handgun.

Sandy says, "I'm tired of that lying, cheating bastard beating me. I'm glad I shot him."

The trooper takes the handgun from her. The other three troopers are standing on the porch.

The first trooper says to the deputy, "I understand that you were having an affair with Sandy, so I cannot allow you to go inside or talk to Sandy. I will also need to have the handguns you have on you for the ballistic test. You are not under arrest. I suggest you remain quiet. A trooper will take you to the sheriff's station, where you can keep track of the progress of this case."

The deputy hands the trooper his service revolver and his backup gun. The deputy says he has a shotgun at his apartment. That will not need to be checked.

The trooper asks for the keys to his apartment. The deputy gives him the keys. A trooper drives him to the sheriff's station. At the same time, another trooper searches the deputy's apartment. No additional weapons were found except for a shotgun.

At the cabin, a trooper asks Sandy if Turk shot the sheriff. Sandy asks when he was shot. She was told three hours ago. Sandy says she is sorry we cannot pin the shooting on Turk, but he has been here since 11 am. No way could he have shot the sheriff.

When the Lieutenant is told what Sandy said about Turk could not have shot the sheriff, he tells the same to the deputy. The deputy says nothing.

Lt. Jackson tells his men at the cabin to take Sandy to the capital to book her. He wants Sandy and Deputy Swanson to refrain from talking to each other.

Lt. Jackson calls ballistics to ask what type of gun was used. They say the weight of the bullet indicates it was a thirty-two. He pulls out the deputy's gun and sees it is also a thirty-two.

He gives the evidence bag with the revolver in it to a trooper to immediately take to the ballistic lab located in the capital.

They have collected 14 guns in the cabin. The handguns will also be taken to the ballistic lab. The other guns will be held in evidence. The troopers must now search the cabin for any evidence of spousal abuse or any other crime.

Chapter 7: Sandy

Sandy Flemington has had a long day; the drive to Springfield, the state's capital, took over an hour. The Central Jail, where Sandy will be held, is an old building, probably built in the late 1940s. It is a large building with almost no windows. The few windows that exist are small and have bars on them. The color is a depressing yellow.

The trooper drove out of his way so Sandy could see the old, cold Central Jail. Fear can bring out the truth in people.

The trooper driving the car says this is where you will stay if the judge decides to hold you for a trial. We are going to the central state police station. You will be allowed to talk to someone about how your husband has mistreated you.

Sandy says the handcuffs are very uncomfortable. The trooper says they will be removed once you are in the station.

Sandy is led to an interview room, where the handcuffs are taken off her. The room looks like every police interview room pictured in a movie or TV show. There is a long table, a few chairs, and a mirror, probably a two-way mirror. She is told if she needs to leave this room, say to use the restroom, the handcuffs will be put back on her.

Alice enters the room; Sandy is told that Alice is an expert in spousal abuse. The trooper leaves. Alice asks Sandy if she is hungry. Sandy says no.

Alice says this will take some time because, in a death case, we need to know everything that has happened. You must be accurate and truthful.

This morning, you were not at the cabin; where were you?

Sandy looks confused; she says "ah" a few times. Her head drops down, and her chin hits her chest.

Alice stares at Sandy for two minutes. Alice says, "At this moment, you are not going to Central Jail; you are going to prison for the rest of your life. Is it true your husband beat you or not?"

Sandy breaks down crying; she keeps saying she is sorry. Alice says nothing for a couple of minutes.

A trooper enters the room, hands Alice a note, and then leaves. The message says, "Sheriff Deputy Herbert Swanson is being held for suspicion of murder."

Alice says in her most authoritative voice, "Where were you? If you do not answer, this will be the last time you will be in a room without bars and a lock."

Sandy is still crying, but Alice knows Sandy hears her.

Sandy quiets down and says, "I want an attorney." Alice asks if she is sure. Sandy says yes. Alice asks, "OK. What is the name of your attorney?"

Sandy says, "I want one of those free attorneys."

Alice says, "You can get an attorney appointed by the court only if you cannot afford one. Can you afford an attorney?"

Sandy asks, "How much does an attorney cost?"

Alice says they usually charge by the hour. The hourly cost can be anywhere from one hundred dollars an hour to several times that amount."

Sandy says, "Wow, I don't think I can afford that."

Alice puts the handcuffs on Sandy. Alice says, "I am placing you under arrest for murder. Everything you say may be taken down and used against you in a court of law. I will now try to get you a court-appointed attorney. This may take an hour or several hours, depending on how fast the court acts and the availability of attorneys. If you lose your case, you may be required to pay your attorney's fees."

Alice loudly says that she needs a trooper in here. In less than a minute, a trooper enters the room. Alice says to book her in a jail cell here in the station.

As Alice leaves the room, she says you can change your mind at any time. She closes the door. Alice pauses outside of the door for a moment. Just as Alice starts to take a step, the door opens, and the trooper steps out and says, "She wants to talk."

Alice walks back into the interview room. Alice tells Sandy, "I need you to say whether you want an attorney now."

Sandy says she has changed her mind and does not want an attorney. OK, let's start again. Where were you this morning, and with whom?"

Sandy says she was with Jeff Swanson at his apartment.

Alice asks, "Who is Jeff Swanson?"

Sandy says, "The brother of Deputy Herbert Swanson.

When was the last time you were with Deputy Herbert Swanson?"

Sandy looks flustered. She tries saying something several times, but no words come out.

Alice thinks it is time to change tactics. Alice says, "I need a trooper in here." In less than a minute, a trooper opens the door.

Alice tells the trooper, "I will be gone between three to four minutes. Please keep Sandy company." Alice turns to Sandy as she walks out the door and says, "I'll be right back."

Five minutes later, Alice returns with a trooper. They both have arms full of food from the station's vending machines, including drinks.

Alice says, "Thank you, troopers." Alice sits down at the table full of junk food. She says to Sandy, "You look hungry; I think your blood sugar is low. You will feel better if you eat something."

Sandy says, "Thank you." Alice thinks, "I got her. Eating together is a bonding activity. She will trust me."

They talk about the food they are eating. Alice will try to ease into the hard questions gently.

Alice asks, "Do you like Greenview?"

Sandy says it is okay.

Alice asks, "How long have you lived there?"

26

Sandy says, "Almost four years."

"When did you meet Deputy Herbert Swanson?"

Sandy says, "The day we moved in. He brought us a welcome basket."

Were you married to Turk when you moved there?"

Sandy says, "We are not married; we were living together when we moved to Greenview. Most people consider us in a common-law marriage."

In comparison, who looks better, Turk or Herb?

Sandys says, Turk.

Alice asks, "Who was better? You know. In bed?" They both giggle.

Sandy says, "Turk. About two years later, Turk started getting off his game. About that time, the Deputy became more fun." They both smirked at each other.

Alice says, "I know what you mean. I had to trade in my old stallion a couple of years ago. It was well worth it. My new guy keeps going and going and going. Just like the Ever-Ready Battery Bunny." They laugh.

Alice says, "Sometimes relationships just run their course." Sandy nods in the affirmative. "So, what happened that you had to shoot Turk."

Sandy says that Turk started beating her about eight months ago. He was having trouble at work, and I think that is why he started hitting me. The first few times, he apologized to me and said he would never do it again.

Did you ever go to the hospital or call the sheriff to have him arrested?

Sandy says she is sorry she did not have him arrested and only got a few bruises, so the hospital visit was unnecessary.

Alice says she believes her, but I need to know who you were with this morning and where you were.

"Herb for an hour, then Herb lent me his car, and I went shopping. There is no Jeff Swanson."

Chapter 8: Deputy Sheriff Herbert Swanson

Since Alice has been talking to Sandy Winters in Springfield, Lieutenant Jackson has been talking to Herb in the Sheriff's office in Greenview. He has been getting constant reports from Alice on what Sandy says.

The Lieutenant and the deputy only talked about unimportant things. Being told that Sandy broke down and told the truth, the Lieutenant takes Alice's lead and asks Herb what he would like for dinner.

Lt. Jackson sends a trooper to pick up the food. Herb had offered, but the Lieutenant said he needed to walk his people occasionally, or they would get feisty. The Lieutenant would not let a prime suspect walk out the door.

While eating, the Lieutenant takes a call from the Forensics Lab. They report the pistol that Sandy Winters had in her hand was the murder weapon of Turk Bowman. The other weapons in the cabin will take some time to run through the FBI database. They have sent the information to the District Attorney's office—the DA plans on filing a first-degree murder charge against Sandy Winters. They also say the deputy's weapons were clean and not involved in the shooting at the sheriff's office.

Lt. Jackson excuses himself. He leaves the dinner table to talk to a trooper. He tells the trooper to get a couple of metal detectors and sweep the area for a mile radius around the sheriff's office looking for pistols. First, check the parking lots around this building. Also, have someone check the dumpsters. Lt. Jackson tells another trooper to check the guns registered by the deputy. Lt. Jackson wants to ensure we have all of the deputy's weapons.

THE O MURDER

Lt. Jackson sits back down at the dinner table. He says to the deputy, "Sandy is being charged with first-degree murder."

The deputy's face quickly changes expressions. The deputy was trying to hide his concern.

Lt. Jackson asks, "Why do you think she killed Turk?"

The deputy stumbles through his words for several seconds, then says, "She says ..."

The Lieutenant interrupts him, shakes his head no, and says, "No. You know why. If you lie to me during a murder investigation, it means you will go to jail. Please take a deep breath and think about staying out of jail."

The deputy lays his head on the table's edge with a thump; looking down at the floor, he cries, "I had no idea she would do something like that."

Lt. Jackson softly says, "I need you to recall every conversation you had with Sandy about Turk. But first, tell me what happened today in this office."

The deputy says, "About mid-morning, the Sheriff gets a call from Turk saying Sandy is missing. Expressing his dismay about going out in a blizzard, the Sheriff leaves for the Turk cabin. I am concerned that Sandy is missing, so I called her cell phone. There was no answer.

The sheriff gives me a report. He does not know if it is a crime scene or just horny people running around. He asked me to call Emma Johnson since she knows who is doing what to whom.

I called Emma, and she showed up about ten minutes later. I introduced her to the Sheriff, and I went to the restroom. About a minute later, I was in the middle of a significant bowel movement when I heard two shots. After about twenty seconds, I exited the bathroom. They were both lying there in a pool of blood. I thought they were both dead, so I ran out the door to see if anybody was around.

I saw a man standing outside the window, looking into the window and on his phone. I know who he is, but I have forgotten his name. I think it was Michael something.

I saw a truck disappear over the hump in the road. I thought it looked like Turk's truck. I drove to Turk's place and watched the cabin to see if anything suspicious was going on. Later you called me on the radio.

What make is Turk's truck?

1955 Ford F150. He put a lot of work into it, keeping it primo.

How many old Ford F150s are around here?

Most people who live around here have an older truck.

Can you create a list of everyone who has an older truck from around here?

Nope. That would be a big list.

Lt. Jackson says, "OK. Contact the DMV and have them send us a list of trucks registered in Greenview."

The deputy says he will do that tomorrow.

Lt. Jackson asks, "How long have you been seeing Sandy?" The deputy says four or five months. This is a very dull town; there is not much else to do in Greenview.

Lt. Jackson says, "I'm not here to judge you; I just want the facts. Tell me about conversations you had with Sandy where she talked about Turk.

The deputy says most of the conversations were about how he mistreated her. That he did not respect her or what she did for him.

The Lieutenant asks, "Was there any physical violence?"

The deputy says, At first, I thought he did assault her. I suggested that I arrest him for assault. She said no, it was emotional assault or just shoving her around. After that, I did not ask if Turk was hurting her; I just assumed that she was exaggerating what Turk was doing. I am shocked that she shot him.

Lt. Jackson asks, "Was there any physical signs that she was physically injured?"

"No."

The Lieutenant asks, "How do you explain Sandy killing Turk?"

"I'm completely shocked that she shot him. It makes no sense to me at all."

Lt. Jackson sends a short text to Alice saying the Deputy says he does not think Turk physically attacked Sandy.

Alice thinks Sandy will go to prison for the rest of her life.

Chapter 9: Oliver

With his peculiar social skills, Oliver earned the moniker "Oliver the Freak" among the townspeople. In his early years, he had been marked by an unusual circumstance that set him apart from his peers. Contrary to common assumptions, wolves did not raise Oliver, but the tales surrounding him painted a different picture.

Despite being able to read and write at a third-grade level, Oliver's communication skills were limited. He could sometimes talk, yet his interactions left others feeling uneasy. His presence alone was enough to make people divert their paths, avoiding any potential encounters with the mysterious figure Oliver the Freak.

Rumors and stories circulated throughout the town, each attempting to explain the circumstances that led to Oliver's peculiar demeanor. Some claimed he had been abandoned in the woods as a child and taken in by a pack of wolves, while others believed he possessed a unique connection with the wild creatures that shaped his identity. Regardless of the truth, Oliver became a subject of fascination and fear in the close-knit community.

As Oliver navigated the town's streets, his presence constantly reminded him of the unknown and the mysteries that shrouded his upbringing. Though perhaps unkind, the nickname encapsulated the collective sentiment of the townspeople who struggled to understand the enigmatic figure that was Oliver the Freak. The stories surrounding him only added to the intrigue, turning Oliver into a living legend within the confines of the small town, where the boundaries between reality and folklore blurred in the shadow of the peculiar young man.

The grass blade by grass blade search of Greenview for the murder weapon turned up two nine-millimeter and one forty-five handgun.

While two troopers were searching a dumpster for handguns, a trooper looked up from his disgusting duty to see a shape come towards them.

The trooper pulls out his handgun and yells, "Halt! We are police officers." The figure keeps moving toward the dumpster. The other trooper in the dumpster stood up from the goo and pulled his weapon.

The figure looked like a highly deformed figure. He was pulling a weapon from his waste. The first trooper yells halt again. Then he yells, "Hold your fire."

The second trooper was about to pull the trigger when the first trooper yelled not to fire.

The figure is waving the handgun at them. The first trooper tries to exit the dumpster with dignity. He falls on his butt. Sitting on the ground, drenched in goo, he says, "I am Trooper Williams; we are looking for a handgun that was thrown away. May I have that gun, please?"

The figure hands the handgun to the trooper, barrel first; the troopers sighs once the figure releases his grip from the pistol. The Trooper Williams pulls out a clean evidence bag and puts the gun in it. All he wants to do now is stand in a shower for a few hours.

Trooper Williams calls in, saying they have found a handgun given to them by a person of limited intelligence. They need some sheets in their patrol car so the goo all over them does not turn the patrol car into a dumpster. He also asks for another patrol car to transport a person of interest to the sheriff's office.

Lt. Jackson asks the deputy, "Is there a deformed person that lives around here?"

The deputy says, "Oliver. I've only briefly seen him once."

The Lieutenant sends a message to Alice to ask Sandy if she was with Oliver this morning."

A few minutes later, Alice sends a note saying Sandy feels sorry for Oliver. She always treated him kindly. But she did not remember seeing him this morning. This could be a bonding between the two since disfigured individuals usually do not receive kindness. I think Oliver should be a person of interest in the sheriff's office shooting. He may have thought he was protecting Sandy for some reason.

The Lieutenant responds to Alice and says let's see what Forensic says.

Bang, the outside door slams open, almost shattering the glass in the door. A man in a suit yells, "What in the hell is going on here? Where is my sheriff staff?"

The deputy smiles and says that the man is the mayor of Greenview. The Lieutenant asks the deputy to talk to him; we are swamped. If he is not happy with that response, we will be glad to throw him in jail for interfering with a homicide investigation.

The deputy talks to the mayor. The mayor leaves in a huff.

Oliver shows up with a trooper. He asks the deputy if there is any place in town to get him some decent clothes. The deputy calls the owner of the General Store. He comes over to the sheriff's office. The Lieutenant tells him that Oliver needs to be fully clothed with a coat, shirt, shoes, socks, pants, and underwear.

The store owner says he will return in fifteen minutes, but Oliver must be cleaned before trying on clothes.

Lt. Jackson asks the forensic people to do a paraffin test on Oliver before he goes into the shower. The forensic team says it might have detected gunpowder on Oliver's hand. If so, it might mean he is the shooter, or he shot it when playing with the gun. The test will be sent to Springfield to confirm the test results.

The paraffin test is not usually used because it can be easily defeated by washing your hands. Everyone who has seen Oliver knows he has yet to wash his hands.

The Lieutenant orders a couple of troopers to take Oliver to the showers in the back room. He then asks the deputy to get a barber to care for Oliver's hair.

The store owner comes back with several pieces of clothing. Oliver is already getting a haircut. The barber lives next door upstairs. The store owner finishes his work and leaves. The Lieutenant asks Oliver if throwing out his old clothes would be ok.

Oliver searches his pockets and pulls out some small rocks. In another pocket, he pulls out a small tube of red paint and a small paintbrush.

A trooper gives an excited, "Lieutenant!"

The Lieutenant says that he sees it. He says to have Forensics take a sample of the paint and compare it to the circle in Turk's cabin.

The Lieutenant orders some food for Oliver. He then asks Oliver where he got the gun?"

"I found it."

Where did you find it?

"Where did I pick it up."

The Lieutenant says, "OK. Let's get Oliver fed, and then we will look for where he found the gun."

Oliver eats slowly but gratefully. He points to the Lieutenant and says he is as nice as Sandy.

The Lieutenant asks, "Did you see Sandy this morning?

"Yes, I waved, but she did not wave back."

The Lieutenant asks, "Did you paint the red circle at the cabin where Sandy lives?"

"Yes, it is pretty, like Sandy."

A trooper asks if he still wants Forensics to check the paint.

Lt. Jackson says that we need to confirm all details of this crime. The Lieutenant then quickly and quietly tells all of the troopers not to mention murder to Oliver. We do not want to spook him.

Lt. Jackson asks Oliver to go for a ride with two troopers. We want to find where you found that gun.

Oliver says OK. Oliver leaves with two troopers.

Forensics calls and says the gun that Oliver had was the gun used in the shooting at the sheriff's office. They say they are running a search for the owner of the gun. We could not lift viable prints from the gun, but an expert on multiple prints will be in tomorrow; maybe we will get a print then.

Lt. Jackson asks the forensic lab if they checked the bullets in the weapon for prints. They said, "Oops, we will do that right now." The Lieutenant curses, almost shouting, and says, "Open the entire weapon and search for prints inside it!"

Everyone in the office was half staring at the Lieutenant. He never curses. The Lieutenant takes a deep breath and slowly exhales. Everyone in the office relaxes.

Twenty minutes later, forensics calls and says we got good prints on the bullets and inside the gun when we field stripped it. They are trying to match the prints. Lt. Jackson says he will fingerprint everyone here, and they should get a set of Sandy's prints in the computer system since she has been arrested. All troopers at the office and the deputy had been fingerprinted when Oliver returned without finding the location where Oliver found the gun. Oliver and the two troopers were then fingerprinted. All of the prints were sent to the State Police computer. Forensics was called, and they were told to check the prints now on the computer.

Lt. Jackson asks the Deputy where your vehicle is. The deputy said that Sandy never gave it back to him. The Lieutenant calls Alice and thinks we must check out the deputy's car. We believe Sandy was the last person to drive it. Please ask her where the vehicle is located.

Ten minutes later, Alice calls back. On the advice of counsel, Sandy now refuses to say anything to us. I will ask her lawyer about the vehicle when he returns tomorrow morning.

Chapter 10: Sheriff Smith of Greenview

Despite the initial allure of a new adventure in a small town, Jack Smith found that being the sheriff was not as fulfilling as he had hoped. The once-beloved Captain from the bustling city of Chicago struggled to adjust to the town's slower pace and limited intellectual stimulation.

Jack Smith grew up in the projects. Abandoned by his father, his mother worked two full-time jobs. In his late teens, he fell in love with Lisa, the most beautiful girl in the world, according to Jack.

Across roads in his life happened when a gang member killed Lisa. Jack tried to buy a gun but was caught by a minister. Instead of sending him to the police, he was put in a program that helped disadvantaged youths. He was shown that by using the law, he could right the wrongs in the world.

At age eighteen, he entered the police academy and stayed in the police force until he retired.

Jack had grown accustomed to the fast-paced, high-stakes law enforcement environment in his twenty-eight years of city living. The quiet town offered a stark contrast, and Jack felt a sense of monotony settling in. The lack of close connections with the locals and the perceived absence of intellectual engagement left him contemplating whether this new chapter of his life was worth continuing.

Jack's disappointment grew as he reflected on his time as the sheriff. Unlike the camaraderie he experienced in the Chicago Police Department, the small town offered little in terms of meaningful relationships. The community's apparent lack of intellectual depth added to his sense of isolation, leaving him questioning whether this venture was the right choice.

As the one-year mark approached, Jack found himself at a crossroads. The prospect of quitting and embarking on a global journey again tempted him. The desire for excitement and a more stimulating environment tugged at him, challenging the notion of settling in an increasingly alien place.

Despite the lackluster experience, Jack knew that decisions about his future needed careful consideration. The once-celebrated Captain weighed the options before him — the familiarity of the city or the uncertainty of a life on the road. As he pondered the choices ahead, Jack couldn't help but reflect on the winding journey that had led him from the bustling streets of Chicago to the quiet solitude of a small-town sheriff.

One day, Jack saw an older lady slip on a broken step on the sidewalk. She looked like she was in great pain. He told her he would be right back with his patrol car. Someone else sat down next to her to keep her company. Jack Smith thought that was a nice thing for that stranger to do.

Jack drove the car to her. The stranger helped her into the car. He said he would come along if the sheriff wanted. The stranger said his name is Dan Young, and he had lived in Greenview most of his life.

Dan filled in the lady's name, Ula Waters, and said she was a widow from the Vietnam War. He told Jack about her hobbies and where she could be found most of the time.

The sheriff says it sounds like you two are close friends. Dan said, "No. We happen to live in Greenview. I hardly know her."

The sheriff remained quiet for the rest of the drive to the hospital. He was trying to understand what Dan meant about just living in Greenview.

The sheriff was sitting in the waiting room with Dan. A doctor came out to talk to him. The doctor asked the sheriff if she was Ula's family member or friend. The sheriff said he is just the sheriff at Greenview, and she lives in Greenview. The doctor says, "Wow, all the cops do in my town is give out speeding tickets."

THE O MURDER

The doctor said she had no broken bones but would stay overnight for observation and probably be released tomorrow. The sheriff told Ula to call the Sheriff's office when they were ready to release her, and they would pick her up and take her home.

The next day, the Sheriff filled in the deputy about Ula Waters calling in for a ride. He said he had some work to do and would return in about half an hour.

The sheriff drove over to where Ula hurt herself on the broken step. He pulled out his tools and started working on the steps. As he worked, people would stop by and talk briefly.

The sheriff thought this would never happen in Chicago; I would not be out fixing a step, nor would strangers stop by for polite conversation. This is much more enjoyable than busting some scum criminal.

Now he understood about Greenview. He started eating every day at the restaurant, even though he did not enjoy the food, he always enjoyed the company. In a few weeks, the Sheriff had met most of the people in Greenview. Before helping Ula, he had only met a handful of the people in the nearly year he lived in Greenview.

Chapter 11: Dragnet

The morning after finding Oliver, the deputy works on the list of people in the area who have a truck, like Turks. The deputy used the DMV database, the internet, and his knowledge of automobiles. By noon, the deputy has his list.

Lt. Jackson looks at the fifty-two pages of the report. Each page was a report of one person. Not only was it a list of people to talk to, with name, address, any known problems the sheriff department had with him, and description of the truck (make, color, year), but also how that person came to be included on the list.

Lt. Jackson thinks to himself, "Wow. I could use somebody like the deputy on my team if he is not the murderer."

There will be ten two-person teams, Lt. Jackson says to his staff. We are looking for a murder suspect. So caution is of premium concern. Everyone must wear their bulletproof vests. When knocking on their door, one trooper must be out of sight of the door with his hand on the gun. Do not go inside their home; we do not know what is inside.

Tell the person you are questioning that you are with the state police, asking for his help in the investigation of the shooting at the sheriff's office. A truck similar to their vehicle was seen driving close to the sheriff's office after the shooting. The shooting was at noon yesterday. If they were there, what did they see? Record their responses.

The populace here may be averse to answering any questions. Push a little, but we do not want a fight because they think their rights are violated. You will not be running into any lawyers. Do not lecture them about the law.

The State Police teams are sent out to do their job. Several people on the list are away because they are at work.

One hour later, a call came in, "Shots fired. Officer down." The Lieutenant sends all patrol cars to the location of the shooting. An ambulance is also sent and told to hold a quarter mile from the site until the shooting scene is cleared.

Several telephone calls came into the sheriff's office reporting multiple gunshots. Ten minutes later, a state trooper calls in, saying the area is contained, to send the ambulance.

The shooter is down with a severe injury, and Trooper Davis was shot in the chest. He may have a broken rib. Bulletproof vests work, but they are not perfect. It is not unusual to have a fractured rib when a shot is received directly into the chest. He is going to the hospital in a patrol car.

Lt. Jackson, concerned about more of his officers getting shot by rednecks, orders all troopers to return to the sheriff's office.

All of the troopers have returned to the sheriff's office except for Trooper Davis (who was shot) and two troopers to watch him and two troopers to secure the shooter at the hospital.

The troopers all report that almost everyone they talked to was belligerent and unhelpful.

The Lieutenant reviewed the few reports that his people recorded.

Chapter 12: Evening Watch

The Lieutenant has lost track of how many troopers he has stationed in Greenview. He had convinced the deputy and Oliver to sleep at the jail without having to arrest them. He would probably not get more information if he had arrested them.

The evening watch was on duty, meaning most troopers had gone to a hotel about ten miles away to eat and sleep.

Lt. Jackson is writing his to-do list for tomorrow.

Item 1. Find the deputy's car.

The deputy had given his car's make, model, and license number. The lieutenant had already put an APB (All Points Bulletin) on the vehicle. In the morning, he will have several patrol cars search the area for the deputy's car.

Item 2. Locate where Oliver found the gun.

Two troopers went out with Oliver, but they could not determine where he found the gun.

Item 3. Get the forensics test results.

Several tests are being done; some can take several days. A little push on the forensics department may speed them up.

Item 4. Find a motive for the shootings.

Maybe Emma was the prime target; since she was a busybody, maybe she pushed someone the wrong way or extorted money from someone to stay quiet. Or the deputy who was involved with Sandy was concerned about Sandy/Turk and shot the Sheriff to cover Sandy's actions. Or Oliver shot the Sheriff, thinking he was protecting Sandy. Or there is someone else who is the murderer.

Item 5. Hold a news conference.

City Hall is the only place in town capable of holding the populist of Greenview; they could help. The Lieutenant will not disclose the suspects.

Chapter 13: News Conference

With one of his troopers shot, the Lieutenant needs to emphasize his troopers must be able to talk to people without puting their lives in jeopardy. The Lieutenant asks the deputy to call the town's Mayor to set up a news conference in city hall. We need the mayor to inform the people about the meeting and ask all citizens to attend tomorrow night.

The mayor gives the Deputy a lot of huff about how the Lieutenant treated him. The Deputy apologized on behalf of the Lieutenant. The Mayor said he would set up the conference for 8 pm and ensure Greenville citizens knew about it.

Probably everyone from town would attend. They all have been concerned about the sheriff's condition, and there is nothing else to do in town.

The town hall started to fill up an hour early.

At 8 pm, the Lieutenant walks into the town hall. There was a mixture of Boos, clapping, and talk.

Lt. Jackson says, "Good evening. Currently, the sheriff's condition is stable, but he is still in critical condition. This means he is still in a condition where he could lose his life." A noise of sympathy goes through the crowd.

The Lieutenant continues, "Sandy Flemington has been arrested for First Degree Murder of Turk Bowman. We have over seventy people we would like to talk to, but one of my troopers was shot trying to ask a few questions. We need these questions answered so we can help narrow down the suspect's list to find the murderer and the person who shot the sheriff." By his tone, everyone knew the Lieutenant was mad.

"The Deputy reported seeing a truck, possibly a 1955 Ford F150. We need to talk to that person to see if they saw anything that will help us find the murderer."

"My trooper who was shot has three kids and a wife who is ill. He is their only means of support. He was trying to ask some questions. He was doing his job, trying to help this community."

"If you have direct knowledge, please come to the sheriff's office. If you have a guess or thought you figured it out, PLEASE do not tell us. We do not have time to listen to your ideas."

"If you do not want us here. We will leave and let the killer kill more of you. In other words, if another of my officers is shot, we leave." There is considerable mumbling from the crowd.

Lt. Jackson left City Hall without speaking to anyone. There is loud talking, some good, some bad.

The mayor takes the opportunity to seize the microphone.

The mayor says, "I know the Lieutenant is a busy man.

He once offered me the chance to put me in jail if I did not leave him alone. Everyone laughs; they know how much he likes to talk.

The mayor announced that new construction to bring a highway through town would start in a few days. Nobody cares that he is pocketing money through his construction company.

In mid-sentence, people start to walk out. The new conference is over.

Chapter 14: Good Lead

Lt. Jackson calls the hospital to check the sheriff's condition. They refuse to tell him because the hospital was ordered not to give his condition to anyone. Lt. Jackson called the State Police main office and got the cell phone number of one of the troopers guarding the sheriff. He calls the trooper; there is no change in the sheriff's condition (he is still in critical condition).

Hungry, Lt. Jackson calls Mary at the restaurant to see if she is still open. She tells him to come over; she will happily cook something for you.

As the Lieutenant stands up to leave, he asks the three troopers on duty if they want anything from the restaurant. They immediately said no. The restaurant has a reputation, and the "Art of Culinary Disappointment" title was well-earned.

The Lieutenant thinks, "My troopers are well educated, with plenty of adjectives, when needed."

Lt. Jackson sits at the counter in the restaurant. He gives his order.

Mary asks how the investigation is going. Lt. Jackson says he cannot comment on most of the inquiry since it is ongoing. We did arrest Sandy for Turk's murder. We are not sure why she shot Turk.

Lt. Jackson asks, "Did Emma have any enemies?"

Mary says that most people loved her, even though she was nosy. The only person she was not friends with was Louis Chats. Emma told Louis his wife was having an affair with Baseball Joe. Mary does not remember his name, but most people call him Baseball Joe.

Lt. Jackson asks, "Does Louis drive a truck?"

"Yes."

"Is it a truck similar looking to the one Turk drove?"

"Yes."

Lt. Jackson says, "Thank you for the food." And he runs out the door. Mary had not finished cooking his order. Mary finishes the Lieutenant's order. And takes it to him at the sheriff's office.

Lt. Jackson remembers there was a report today on Louis Chats. He finds the paperwork on Chats. He said he was out of town yesterday and just returned from Los Angeles. He needed to find out where his ticket stub was located.

The Lieutenant tells a trooper to get a search warrant for Louis Chats. He orders another trooper to see if there are any recent flights that Louis Chats took.

Lt. Jackson wakes the deputy and asks him what he knows about Louis Chats. Stunned, the deputy first says, "What?" Then he fully wakes and shouts, "YES!"

The deputy says that Louis used to be a very likable guy until he divorced his wife. After that, he turned into a mean, angry man. Nearly every month, I would get a report of him doing something mean.

The deputy asks, "How did you figure it out?

Lt. Jackson says, "We were searching for why the sheriff was shot, then it came to me we should also look at the possibility that the shooter was after mainly Emma and not the sheriff. I asked Mary if Emma had any enemies. Mary told me about Louis.

I put in a search warrant request to the judge. When we get the warrant, would you like to come along?

The deputy says, "Yes, Yes, Yes! Thank you so very much."

Lt. Jackson asks a trooper to see if Louis Chats is a registered gun owner. Ten minutes later, the trooper reports that Louis owns a thirty-two with the same serial number as the murder weapon.

"Oliver is still a suspect. Oliver may have gotten/stolen the gun from Louis," Lt. Jackson thinks; the deputy is still a suspect.

The Lieutenant tells the Deputy we will execute a search tomorrow morning, that this is not absolute proof, and we have other suspects. Try to go back to sleep; you will want to be well-rested for tomorrow.

The Lieutenant's list of suspects:

Louis Chats
Has a strong motive. Has a means. And he had the opportunity.

Oliver
Has a possible motive. He had the means. He may have had the opportunity.

Sandy
She did kill Turk (99.9% possibility she killed Turk)—unknown motive.
She might have had the gun.
She may have had the opportunity.

Deputy Herbert Swanson
He had a motive.
He may have had means.
He had the opportunity.

Turk
Unknown if he had a motive.
He may have had means.
He might have had an opportunity.

The Person in the Shadows
There may be somebody or somebodies that we have yet to identify.

Seventy-two people have a truck like the one leaving the scene of the shooting at the sheriff's office.

No known Motive, Means, or Opportunity.

THE O MURDER

The Lieutenant writes that there is a big piece of the puzzle that I am missing.

One or more of the suspects might have done it, or there is someone else. Occam's Razor: The simplest answer is the most likely solution.

The Lieutenant thinks he has a town where nearly one-third of the people are suspects. It is time to reduce the number of parameters that define a suspect or start over from the beginning. I may take the truck out of the equation.

Chapter 16: Louis Chats

Louis, a quiet and unassuming man, had always been an outsider in the close-knit community of Greenview. With his unremarkable looks and a demeanor that blended seamlessly into the background, he seldom attracted attention. Some believe his personality came from growing up as an only child who lived out of town with no friends.

His professional life mirrored his personal one — Louis worked as an accountant, diligently crunching numbers with a precision that matched his punctuality. Despite being a dependable employee, his colleagues often found him to be a bit dull and uninteresting. He adhered to a routine, never deviating from his predictable path.

However, Louis's life took an unexpected turn when his co-worker Emma shattered the tranquility surrounding him. She revealed the painful truth about his wife's infidelity. In the face of this betrayal, Louis's response was swift and decisive. He immediately filed for divorce, severing ties with his unfaithful wife and shutting himself off emotionally from her and the world.

Louis initially harbored resentment towards Emma for bringing such distressing news into his life, but his feelings evolved. The intense hatred gradually led to cynicism. He became withdrawn, finding solace in his work and rarely engaging in social interactions.

Louis's transformation was evident in his newfound reluctance to connect with others. He now viewed relationships through skepticism, doubting the sincerity of human connections. Conversations became a means to an end for him, reserved solely for acquiring information essential to his work. The once-boring man became an enigma, navigating the complexities of life with a guarded heart, haunted by the scars of betrayal and marked by a profound sense of detachment.

Chapter 17: The Warrant

The Lieutenant was sure Louis Chats was the shooter. They received a warrant to search Louis's home for any papers relating to plane tickets and his feelings about Emma and the Sheriff.

Lt. Jackson would arrest Louis no matter what they found in his home.

The twenty troopers and the deputy waited in the office for instructions from the Lieutenant.

The Lieutenant walks into the main area with a smile on his face. He says we will have five troopers in each location: the back, the right side, the left side, and the front of his house. The deputy and I will knock on the front door.

If the suspect brandishes a weapon, "Do not fire."

If the suspect shoots, "Do not fire unless he is directly shooting at you or a fellow trooper." Lt. Jackson handed the deputy a bulletproof vest and said everyone must wear their vest.

"It is 7:30 am. The suspect does not leave for the office until 8 am. The suspect will be in his home. It is believed the suspect will not offer any resistance. You all have your assigned places. Let's be careful, and no shooting unless absolutely necessary."

The twenty troopers leave in an orderly fashion, with stern looks on their face.

The Lieutenant will leave in five minutes to give the troopers time to get set in their positions. The deputy is nervous. The Lieutenant did not return the deputy's weapons. He did not want an unknown entity on this simple raid.

The Lieutenant arrives in his patrol car with his red lights flashing. They leave the vehicle, the Lieutenant leaving his red lights on. They walk to the front door. The deputy feels like the walkway is miles long.

The Lieutenant instructs the deputy to stand on the grass, putting the deputy out of the line of fire. The Lieutenant rings the doorbell.

A meek voice from the other side asks who it is. Lt. Jackson answers, "Lieutenant Jackson of the state police and Deputy Swanson. Please open the door."

The voice says, "Why?"

"Open the door, or we will knock down the door. You will probably be harmed. We have a search warrant for your home. Your house is surrounded. Please open the door now. This is your last warning."

Louis opens his door. The five troopers immediately pushed into his house and went through any papers they could find.

The Lieutenant says to have a seat. The search will take some time. Louis sits in the chair. The Lieutenant sees that there is food in the kitchen being cooked. He has a trooper turn off the stove.

There are now ten troopers searching his home. The Lieutenant sends the rest back to the office.

After thirty minutes of searching, no interesting papers were found.

The Lieutenant sits beside Louis and says, "We would like you to come to the sheriff's office with us."

Louis asks, "Why?"

"We have questions about the shooting at the sheriff's office we would like you to answer." Says the Lieutenant.

"Do I have to go?"

"If you do not volunteer to go with us, I will arrest you, put you in handcuffs, and lead you to my car. If you come freely, you can sit in the front seat, and there will be no handcuffs."

"OK, I will go freely to the office."

The drive to the office could have been more uneventful. Several citizens were waiting outside the sheriff's office; word about the raid on Louis's home had gotten out.

THE O MURDER

Louis was hesitant about getting out of the patrol car. The Lieutenant said, "Everything is OK," and extended his hand to help Louis out of the car."

There are mumblings in the crowd. One person shouts, "Murderer!" The Lieutenant gives the public a stern stare that would quiet anyone with evil intent.

The Lieutenant and Louis sit in the sheriff's personal office, which has windows as walls. A camera was set up and running in the office.

Lt. Jackson says, "The ballistic report says your .32 pistol was the pistol used in this office shooting."

Louis says, "That is not possible. It was stolen three months ago."

Lt. Jackson shouts, "Deputy!"

The Deputy runs into the office. The Lieutenant tells him that Louis's handgun was stolen three months ago. "GET ME THE CASE FILE!"

The deputy says, "Yes, sir." And leaves the office in a run.

"The shooting was at noon; where were you when the shooting happened."

"Here."

The Lieutenant almost faints from frustration. "Do you mean in this office? You said earlier that you were in Los Angeles."

"I lied because they disturbed me earlier by asking questions. No, I was at the restaurant across the street. Most of the people from my office were there. Most of us came out to the street when someone said they heard gunshots."

"Who were you sitting next to?"

"I was sitting by myself."

Highly suspicious, the Lieutenant orders a trooper to make a layout of the tables at the restaurant. He tells the trooper to ask Mary if the design has changed since yesterday and if she remembers who was sitting where then talk to everyone at his office to see where they said they sat.

Louis made a mark where he was sitting on a copy of the restaurant's layout. His location matched what Mary had marked on her copy of his place.

The Lieutenant asks who said they heard a gunshot.

Louis says he does not know.

A trooper asked Mary if she heard a gunshot, and who shouted, "I heard a gunshot."

Mary said she did not hear a gunshot and thought Louis might be the one who shouted, "Gunshot." The Lieutenant took it with a grain of salt. Mary guessed that Louis was the one who shouted.

The Lieutenant assigns two troopers to go to Louis's workplace and ask them about the same setting, gunshot noise, who shouted "gunshot," and if they saw Louis leave from the back door. The restrooms were in the same back hallway as the back door. The court does not like witnesses that guess. I need someone who knows what happened, who shouted, and where Louis was during the meal.

Mary confirms an exit door in the back next to the restrooms.

Chapter 18: Awaken

Sheriff Smith gradually regains consciousness and is surrounded by a hospital room's sterile clinical environment. The throbbing pain in his chest clouds his thoughts, making it difficult for him to recall the events that led him here. He cannot remember what season it is. As he blinks away the haze, the room becomes focused, revealing concerned faces hovering over him.

The attending doctor, a middle-aged man with a serious demeanor, checks Sheriff Smith's vital signs and observes his disoriented state. Sensing the sheriff's struggle to answer questions, the doctor intervenes, signaling the troopers to halt their inquiries temporarily. He advises them that Sheriff Smith needs time to recover before undergoing any further questioning.

Sitting at the sheriff's desk in Greenview, Lt. Jackson received an urgent call from one of the troopers at the hospital. The lieutenant listens intently as the trooper briefs him on the Sheriff's condition. Immediately recognizing the situation's sensitivity, Lt. Jackson emphasizes the gravity of the matter to the trooper.

"This is top secret," Lt. Jackson declares sternly. "The Sheriff's life could be in danger, and we can't risk tipping off the murderer, who may flee or attack the sheriff. We need to handle this with extreme caution." Aware of the potential threats looming, Lt. Jackson dispatches two additional troopers to the hospital for added security.

"Do not suggest any answers to the Sheriff. His present mental condition could make him highly acceptable to answers which are not correct."

"At no time, "the Lieutenant stresses with authority, "will there ever be a minute where a trooper does not have the sheriff in their line of sight. We can't afford any lapses in surveillance. "The lieutenant instructs the two newly assigned troopers to get to the hospital immediately. "Code 3. Use red lights and sirens!"

The two troopers run to their patrol car. They take off with an identified intent, knowing what they do is urgent and necessary.

This murder case will be more straightforward if the sheriff survives—extra energy courses through the two troopers.

Chapter 19: Lawyers

Lt. Jackson was ready to call the DA with everything they needed to convict Louis Chats. The Lieutenant is proud; everyone can see a smile on his face. He says, "We got him," not to anybody in particular.

There is a knock on the office's glass door. The Lieutenant waves the trooper in. He is told the DA is on the phone. The Lieutenant thinks it is perfect timing. Knowing the DA personally, he answers the phone with, "Great news, Jim."

Jim says, "It is great news we got a confession from the shooter for the murder and assault at the sheriff's office."

Lt. Jackson says, "Huh? I don't understand. Who confessed?"

"Sandy Flemington."

Lt. Jackson says, "I believe I have a case that Louis Chats killed Emma Johnson and shot the sheriff."

Jim says, "Send me what you have on Louis Chats. I will review it. I put an agent in Sandy's jail cell, and Sandy confessed everything. We have a minute-by-minute timetable of what she did. Including how she got the gun. And where she threw away the gun she used. I strongly request you release Louis Chats if you have him in custody."

Lt. Jackson says thank you to the DA and hangs up.

The Lieutenant walks to Louis Chats in a jail cell and unlocks the door. He says, "We are going for a ride."

They walk to his patrol car, and the Lieutenant tells Chats to get in the front seat. They drive to Chat's office. The Lieutenant says, "You are not under arrest or under suspicion. We have the person who shot the sheriff and Emma. Please let me go to your office and apologize to you in front of your workers so they have no lingering suspicions."

Louis says that he appreciates the Lieutenant doing that for him.

They walk into the office. There is a gasp from everyone in the office. They all thought he was the murderer.

The Lieutenant says, "I am Lieutenant Jackson. I was in charge of finding the person responsible for the three shootings that happened in this town. The DA agrees that the person responsible for the three shootings was Sandy."

The office erupts in noise, from "No's" being shouted to laughter.

The Lieutenant holds up his hand to quiet the crowd. He continues, "Louis is a courageous man. He answered every question we asked him. He did not request a lawyer or remain silent. When this happens in an investigation, it slows down the speed of the investigation."

"No one but a true American hero would risk being sent to prison for life to help find the dastardly criminal." The Lieutenant hands Louis his business card and says to call him anytime for anything.

The Lieutenant says, "On a personal note: A woman screwed you over. She does it to you every day that you let it upset you. There are many good women out there; take a chance."

The Lieutenant turns and walks out the door to applause.

The Lieutenant sticks his head back into the office and says, "If you need a ride home, please give me a call."

Louis says thank you and does not think it will be a problem.

Lt. Jackson heads back to the sheriff's office to close up shop.

He tells everyone that Sandy has confessed to the shooting in this office. He sends all of their work on Louis to the DA and assigns troopers to return their equipment to their office.

He gives the deputy his guns and tells him this office is all his.

There is a printout of Sandy's confession and how she did it.

Chapter 20: Report on Sandy

The Lieutenant reads the confession.

Sandy nursed an ongoing grudge against the sheriff, a festering resentment ignited by a ticket issued to her a year ago. Unyielding in her belief that her actions were well within the bounds of the law, she went to great lengths to contest the citation. She hired a lawyer and talked to him for two hours (cost: $400). Sandy made her case in court, only to face the bitter taste of defeat when the judge ruled against her.

Sandy's frustration erupted when the guilty verdict was delivered. Sandy, unable to contain her displeasure, directed her ire at the judge, resulting in a near-incarceration for contempt of court. A seemingly inconspicuous illegal parking violation sparked all of this drama. According to Sandy, the alley she parked in wasn't a road, allowing her to block cars from using it.

In her relentless pursuit of justice—albeit for a minor infraction—Sandy sought solace in venting her frustrations to Turk. However, Turk, uninterested in her legal battles, offered no sympathy. His responses were consistently calm, revolving primarily around the pressing matter of whether dinner was ready.

As Sandy's complaints became a daily routine, Turk's lack of engagement remained steadfast. The juxtaposition of Sandy's emotional legal crusade against Turk's culinary concerns created a humorous dynamic.

Fueled by a simmering vendetta against the sheriff, Sandy embarked on an unexpected alliance with the deputy. Although unsure how this newfound relationship would aid her cause, Sandy reveled in the deputy's company, finding solace in the thrill of the unconventional connection.

Casual chit-chat with the deputy unveiled the identity of the suspected thief haunting Greenview. Sandy, seizing an opportunity, knew the thief and acquired a gun from him, uncertain how she would use it.

On the fateful day after a shopping trip, Sandy found herself halted at a stop sign. The sheriff, oblivious to Sandy's brewing resentment, flashed a smile and a wave. Fueled by her frustration over perceived mistreatment, Sandy stewed in her car, thinking about the sheriff's insincere smile.

In a rage, she parked in the back of the office. Sandy retrieved the gun from her purse and stormed into the sheriff's office, where she shot both the sheriff and Emma, the latter being a casualty of personal dislike.

On her way home, Sandy discarded the incriminating weapon in the alley where she received her earlier ticket, relishing a chilling laugh.

The deputy was parked at the bottom of the hill where her cabin sat. To conceal her actions from the deputy, she parked his personal car off the highway to avoid being easily noticed.

Sandy walked through the woods to reach her cabin.

Upon entering the cabin, Sandy's grievances found a new target—Turk. The mundane demands for lunch sparked a heated argument, with Sandy feeling unappreciated for the sacrifices she believed she made for Turk.

A knock at the door, courtesy of the deputy, intensified Sandy's paranoia. Fearing arrest, she hastily armed herself with one of the many guns scattered throughout the cabin. The deputy persisted, demanding entry, and Sandy, now operating on instinct, shot Turk as he reached for the door, relieving the mounting pressure within her.

Sandy opened the door to the persistent deputy in a state of temporary relief. Her disjointed words hung in the air as she was ushered into a patrol car bound for the state capital.

THE O MURDER

Feeling an unexpected sense of relaxation, Sandy reveled in the belief that the sheriff lay dead. Turk's fate seemed inconsequential as she drifted into the uncertain journey ahead.

Chapter 21: Court

Sandy's court-appointed attorney, Allen Stein, told Sandy to say nothing in court. This is only the start of appearing in court. Sandy's head is spinning. She cannot understand what people are saying. She hears noise but cannot make out any words. Everything is a blur.

Allen Stein is excited to work on his first double homicide and possibly a triple homicide if the sheriff does not survive. He can barely control his excitement. He thinks, "Mom will be excited to hear about this case." Sandy's attorney did not notice that Sandy did not look well.

The judge asks if they are ready to plea to the two counts of first-degree murder and the one count of attempted murder.

Allen Stein says we are not ready to enter a plea. He is asking for a psychological exam to be performed before a plea can be entered.

The judge looks at his calendar and says, "In two months, we will visit again; at that time, you will enter a plea."

Sandy collapses to the floor. Sandy is rushed to the hospital. An MRI shows Sandy has a tumor pushing against the Prefrontal cortex. This type of tumor usually causes personality changes.

At his office, Sandy's attorney gets a call from the hospital giving him the news about the brain tumor. He jumps up and yells, "Yippee!" He says he is sorry and hangs up on the hospital. This means his client may get off on the murder charges after she admits to shooting the victims. Allen Stein thinks this may set him for life, winning a case of triple murder.

The next day, Allen Stein gets a call saying that the sheriff is fully conscious and has identified Sandy as the shooter.

Allen Stein thinks, can my day get any worse?

That day, surgeons attempt to remove the tumor. Sandy does not survive the surgery. Allen Stein is depressed. He fights the depression by thinking there are murders all of the time; he will likely get another chance at stardom.

A funeral service is not given for Sandy.

The town of Greenview rejoices when they hear the sheriff is getting better.

Jack, the snowplow guy, goes back to clearing the roads. The few merchants of Greenview shovel the snow in front of their businesses. Louis Chats double-checks his figures and smiles at a pretty girl. Deputy Sheriff Herbert Swanson is acting sheriff with no crime happening. Lt. Jackson moves back to the state capital to fill out reports. The town gives Oliver a small house; it is a death house, and nobody would buy it.

The town goes back to its mode of doing nothing interesting.

Chapter 22: The End

He thinks to himself, "I will wait a year. Then, mayhem happens again; another play I orchestrate will come to life."

Luis Chats has a big smile, "The fusion of Sandy's gullibility and my cunning proved to be a deadly concoction." He introduced the drug into Sandy's meals, gradually entrancing her under his control. Through hypnotic suggestions, Luis fueled her hatred toward specific individuals, even teaching her a trigger word. When uttered, it triggered a disturbing compulsion within Sandy, turning her into a lethal instrument against those she despised.

He smiles at a girl in the office. She looks like a good prospect. She is not intelligent; I'm sure she will be perfect for my next play.

He softly says to himself, "Yes, she will be the shooter; now I need three victims. Maybe the Deputy. He might figure out what happened, so taking him out will protect me."

I will do one more play here, then move to another small town. A small town means the police officers were intellectually challenged (He had a lower chance of getting caught).

Maybe I should make my ex-wife a victim in my next play. It did not upset Louis that she was unfaithful. She was just a prop in a play. The divorce was a reason to be distant from everyone.

Being distant, he could hide in the shadows and be low on the suspect list. No one could question his intelligence; he is more intelligent than everyone. He liked being the puppet master that no one could see.

Louis is excited about writing his new play. He feels the adrenaline surge in his body and pictures in his mind of bloody bodies. But not now; he has accounting work to do.

He will sleep well tonight, knowing he is more intelligent than everyone.

Glossary

Alice is an expert in spousal abuse. She works for the state police. She interviews Sandy.

Allen Stein is the lawyer for Sandy.

Deputy Sheriff Herbert Swanson, Herb, deputy – suspect in murder case.

Greenview – town of 300 citizens.

Jack - the snowplow guy. He does not like snow or cold, but he does his job.

Sandy Flemington, Sandy is a suspect in the murder cases. She is the wife of Turk.

Sheriff Jack Smith, Sheriff Smith, sheriff, is the sheriff of Greenview. He had been a captain of the Chicago Police Department.

Peggy Jackson is the wife of Lieutenant Samuel Jackson.

Trooper Williams – searched in the dumpster, covered in goo, and got the gun used in the shooting of two people.

Turk, Turk Bowman – worked in a slaughterhouse. He was shot and killed by his common-law wife.

Louis Chats is a suspect in a murder case. He is an accountant and has no real friends.

Lt. Jackson of the state police. He headed the murder investigation.

Mary, owner of the restaurant.

The Seventy-Two suspects are townspeople who own a truck similar to the one seen, leaving the shooting of two victims.

--